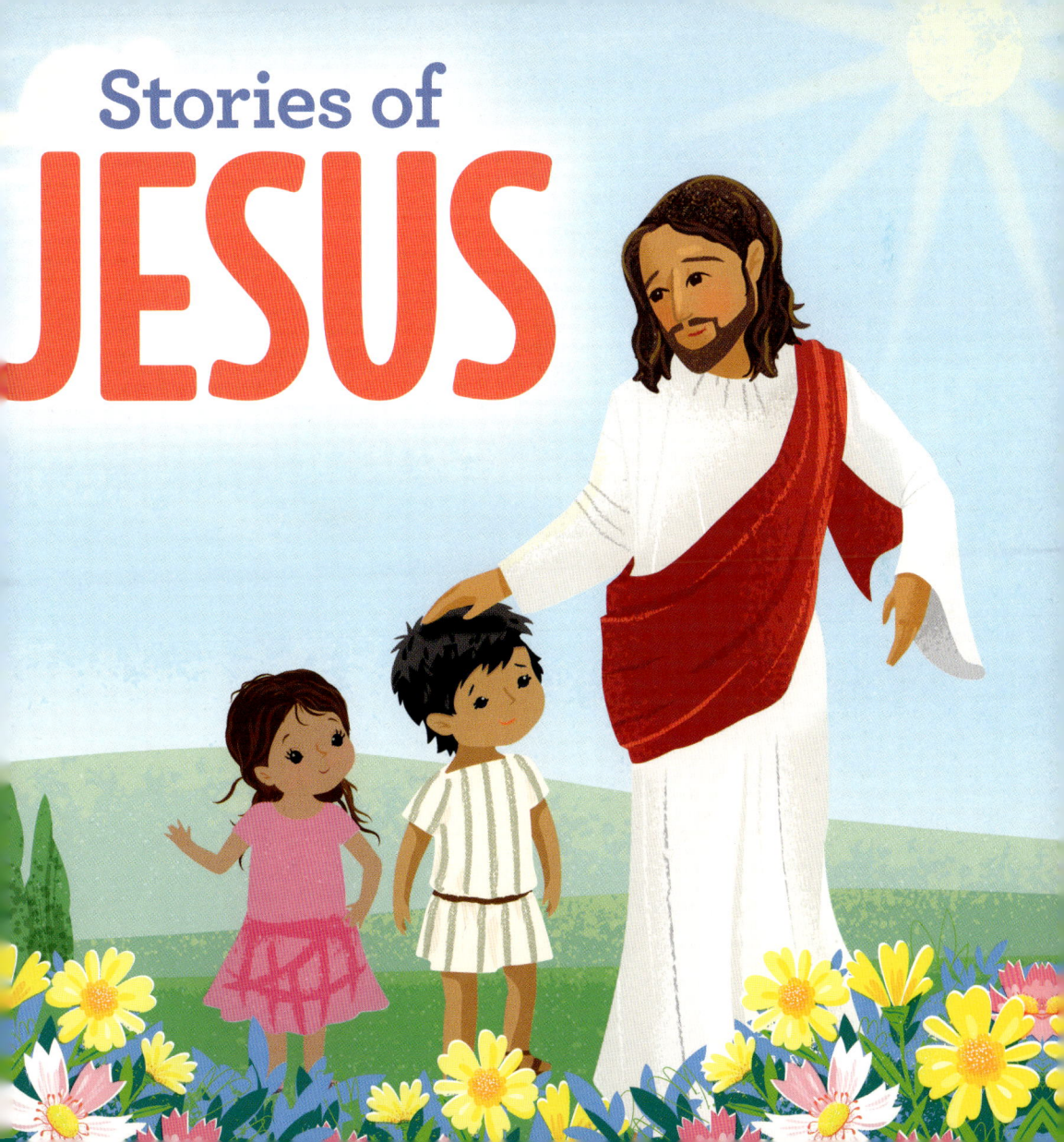

Illustrated by: Stacy Peterson and Dan Crisp

Bible stories adapted by: Beth Taylor

Additional text: traditional hymns, prayers, and folk songs

Scripture quotations from *The Holy Bible, King James Version*

Little Grasshopper Books and Little Grasshopper Library are trademarks of Louis Weber.

© 2023 Publications International, Ltd. All rights reserved.

This publication may not be reproduced or quoted from in whole or in part by any means whatsoever without written permission from:

Louis Weber, CEO
Publications International, Ltd.
8140 Lehigh Avenue
Morton Grove, IL 60053

Permission is never granted for commercial purposes.

For inquiries email: **customer_service@littlegrasshopperbooks.com**

ISBN: 978-1-63938-286-6

Manufactured in China.

8 7 6 5 4 3 2 1

Table of Contents

4	The Birth of Jesus	75	The Lord's Prayer
23	O Little Town of Bethlehem	76	Every Time I Feel the Spirit
24	Away in the Manger	77	Hear Us Pray
26	Joy to the World	78	O How I Love Jesus
27	Hark the Herald Angels Sing	80	What a Friend We Have in Jesus
28	Jesus as a Child	82	The Parables
38	Gentle Jesus	119	The King of Love My Shepherd Is
40	This Is My Father's World	120	My Shepherd Will Supply My Need
42	Jesus's Little Ones	121	Blessed Assurance, Jesus Is Mine
44	John the Baptist	122	Jesus Is the Sweetest Name I Know
50	Wade in the Water	123	Praise God from Whom All Blessings Flow
51	Take Me to the Water	124	The Miracles of Jesus
52	'Tis So Sweet to Trust in Jesus	143	Now Thank We All Our God
53	Give Me Jesus	144	Jesus Is a Rock in a Weary Land
54	Jesus's Followers and Friends	145	Turn Your Eyes Upon Jesus
61	Jesus Loves the Little Children	146	Jesus Saves
62	Jesus Loves Me	148	Jesus Saves Us
63	No Friend Like Jesus	154	When I Survey the Wondrous Cross
64	O the Deep, Deep Love of Jesus	155	Jesus Paid It All
66	Since Jesus Came into My Heart	156	In the Garden
67	I Want Jesus to Walk with Me	158	Jesus Christ Is Risen Today
68	Jesus Teaches	160	I Love to Tell the Story

The Birth of Jesus

Once there was a young woman named Mary who lived in the town of Nazareth. Mary was engaged to be married to a carpenter named Joseph.

One day God sent an angel to give Mary some very important news.

"You will have a baby boy, and you will name him Jesus," the angel said. "He will be the Son of God."

Mary was confused, but she trusted God. Joseph trusted God too. They agreed to take care of God's special son.

Around this time, the emperor in Rome made a law. The law said that everyone must go to their own hometown to register and pay taxes.

Joseph was from Bethlehem, so that is where he had to go. Mary was going to have her baby soon, but she traveled to Bethlehem with Joseph anyway.

Mary and Joseph arrived in Bethlehem at night. All the inns were full.

They stayed in a stable with the animals since there was no other room for them.

Mary's son was born that night. She named him Jesus as the angel told her.

Mary wrapped him in a blanket and placed him in a manger. A bright star shone over the place where Jesus lay.

On that same night, some shepherds were watching over their sheep. An angel appeared. The shepherds were frightened.

"Do not be afraid," the angel said. "I bring you great news. A savior is born in Bethlehem tonight. He is Christ the Lord. You will find him lying in a manger."

Suddenly, the whole sky lit up with many angels. The angels said, "Glory to God and peace on Earth!"

After the angels left, the shepherds said to one another, "Let us go to Bethlehem. Let us find this baby."

The shepherds hurried to Bethlehem. They found Jesus lying in a manger, just as the angel told them.

The shepherds bowed down and worshipped Jesus. After they left, the shepherds told everyone the good news.

Some wise men from far away saw a bright star in the sky. They followed the star all the way to the place where Jesus lay.

The wise men brought Jesus gifts of gold, frankincense, and myrrh. They worshipped Jesus.

An angel warned Joseph in a dream that Bethlehem was not safe for Jesus. The angel said that Egypt was safe. So Joseph, Mary, and Jesus left for Egypt.

O Little Town of Bethlehem

O little town of Bethlehem,
How still we see thee lie!
Above thy deep and dreamless sleep
The silent stars go by.
Yet in thy dark streets shineth
The everlasting light.
The hopes and fears of all the years
Are met in thee tonight.

Away in the Manger

Away in a manger, no crib for a bed,
The little Lord Jesus laid down his sweet head.
The stars in the bright sky looked down where he lay,
The little Lord Jesus asleep on the hay.

The cattle are lowing, the baby awakes,
But little Lord Jesus no crying he makes.
I love you, Lord Jesus. Look down from the sky,
And stay by my side until morning is nigh.

Joy to the World

Joy to the world, the Lord is come!
Let earth receive her King.
Let every heart prepare him room,
And heaven and nature sing,
And heaven and nature sing,
And heaven, and heaven and nature sing.

Hark the Herald Angels Sing

Hark! the herald angels sing,
"Glory to the newborn King!
Peace on earth, and mercy mild,
God and sinners reconciled!"
Joyful, all ye nations, rise,
Join the triumph of the skies.
With the angelic hosts proclaim,
"Christ is born in Bethlehem!"

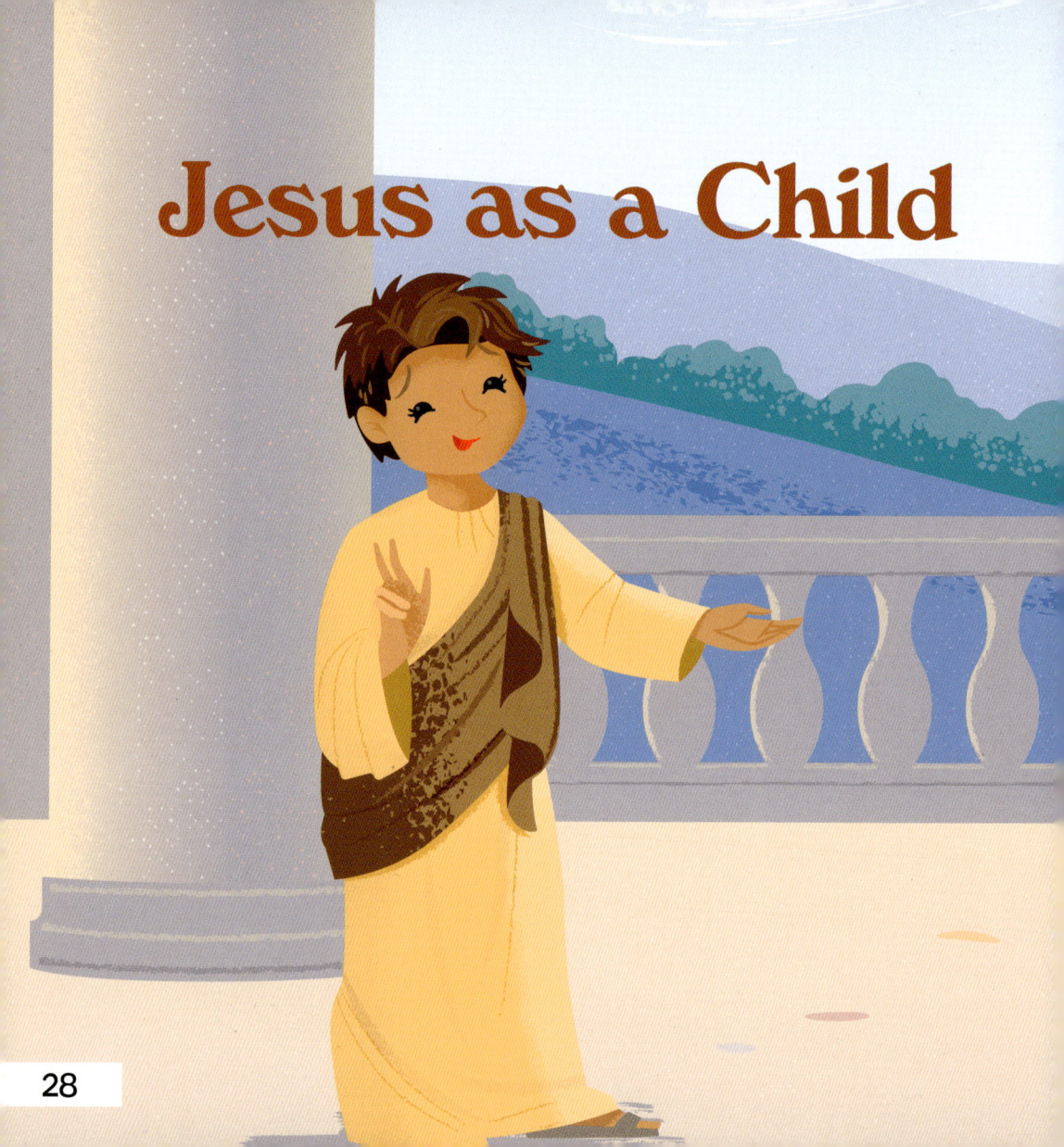

Jesus was a child just like you! He ate, sneezed, and played games. Since Joseph was a carpenter, Jesus probably learned to make things. Jesus grew up hearing stories about the Jewish faith.

Jesus and all the children around him heard about how God created the world. God made the sky and land, the plants and animals, and the people too.

Then God made a man named Adam and a woman named Eve. God gave them a beautiful place to live called the Garden of Eden. Because Adam and Eve sinned, they had to leave the Garden. Jesus came to the world to save people from sin.

Jewish children heard about how God loved and saved the Israelite people. God told the hero Moses to lead them out of Egypt. God performed a miracle that parted the sea so the Israelites could walk on dry land!

God gave Moses two stone tablets with ten special rules.

These rules told people how to love and obey God and how to be good to people around them.

Another hero was David. When David was young, he fought the giant Goliath and won!

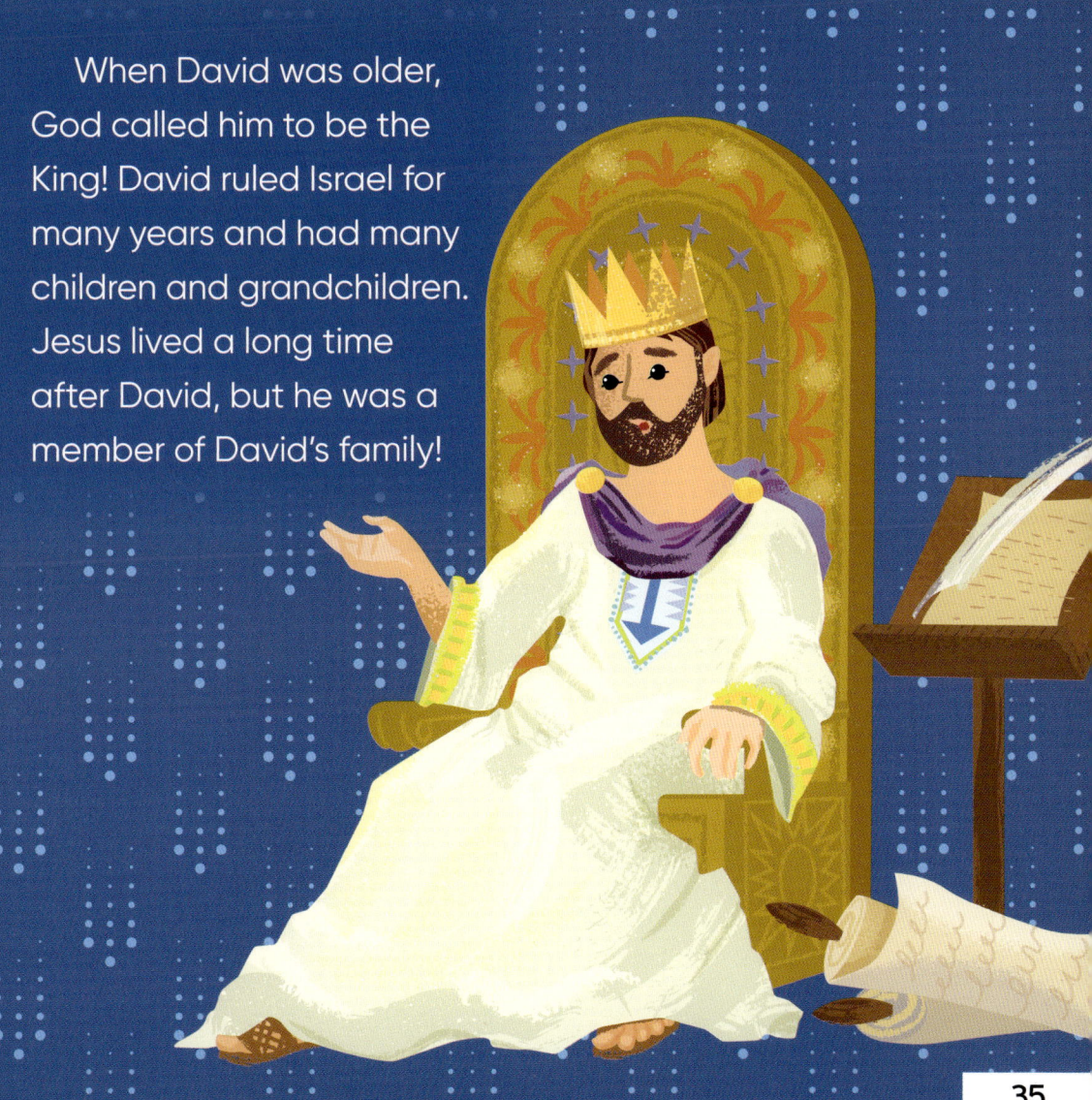

When David was older, God called him to be the King! David ruled Israel for many years and had many children and grandchildren. Jesus lived a long time after David, but he was a member of David's family!

When Jesus was twelve years old, he and his family went to Jerusalem. They celebrated the Jewish feast of Passover to remember how God saved the Jewish people from Egypt. On the way home, Mary and Joseph could not find Jesus.

They went back and found Jesus in the Temple. He was with the teachers, asking them questions and talking about faith. Jesus told Mary and Joseph that he was in his Father's house.

Gentle Jesus

Gentle Jesus, meek and mild,
Look upon a little child.
Pity my simplicity,
Suffer me to come to thee.

Lamb of God, I look to thee.
Thou shalt my example be.
Thou art gentle, meek and mild.
Thou was once a little child.

This Is My Father's World

This is my Father's world,
And to my listening ears,
All nature sings, and round me rings
The music of the spheres.

This is my Father's world,
I rest me in the thought
Of rocks and trees, of skies and seas
His hand the wonders wrought.

Jesus's Little Ones

Jesus's little ones are we,
From all sin he makes us free,
More like him to daily be,
For he loves us so.

Jesus is the truest Friend,
On his strength we can depend,
And his care will never end,
For he loves us so.

In the straight and narrow way
He will lead us day by day,
Seek us if we go astray,
For he loves us so.

John the Baptist

Long ago, there was a man named John. He was Jesus's cousin. Before John was born, the angel Gabriel told John's father that John would be a great man who loved God. John grew up to be a prophet who told people about God.

John lived a simple life in the wilderness. His clothes were made of camel hair. He ate simple meals of locusts and wild honey. God was all he needed.

People came from near and far to hear John speak. He told his followers to feel sorry for their sins and to ask God for forgiveness.

John baptized people. He blessed them and poured water on their heads.

One day John baptized Jesus. A voice from heaven said, "This is my son and I am happy with him."

Wade in the Water

Wade in the water,
Wade in the water, children,
Wade in the water.
God's gonna trouble the water.

Take Me to the Water

Take me to the water,
Take me to the water,
Take me to the water
to be baptized.

I love Jesus,
I love Jesus,
I love Jesus.
Yes, I do.

'Tis So Sweet to Trust in Jesus

'Tis so sweet to trust in Jesus,
And to take him at his word,
Just to rest upon his promise,
And to know, "Thus saith the Lord."

Give Me Jesus

In the morning when I rise,

In the morning when I rise,

In the morning when I rise,

Give me Jesus.

Give me Jesus, give me Jesus.

You may have all this world, give me Jesus.

Jesus's Followers and Friends

When Jesus began to teach and perform miracles, he chose twelve helpers, or disciples. Peter (also called Simon), James, and John were fishermen. When Jesus called them to be disciples, they followed him.

Mary Magdalene was a faithful follower of Jesus. She traveled with Jesus to listen to him teach.

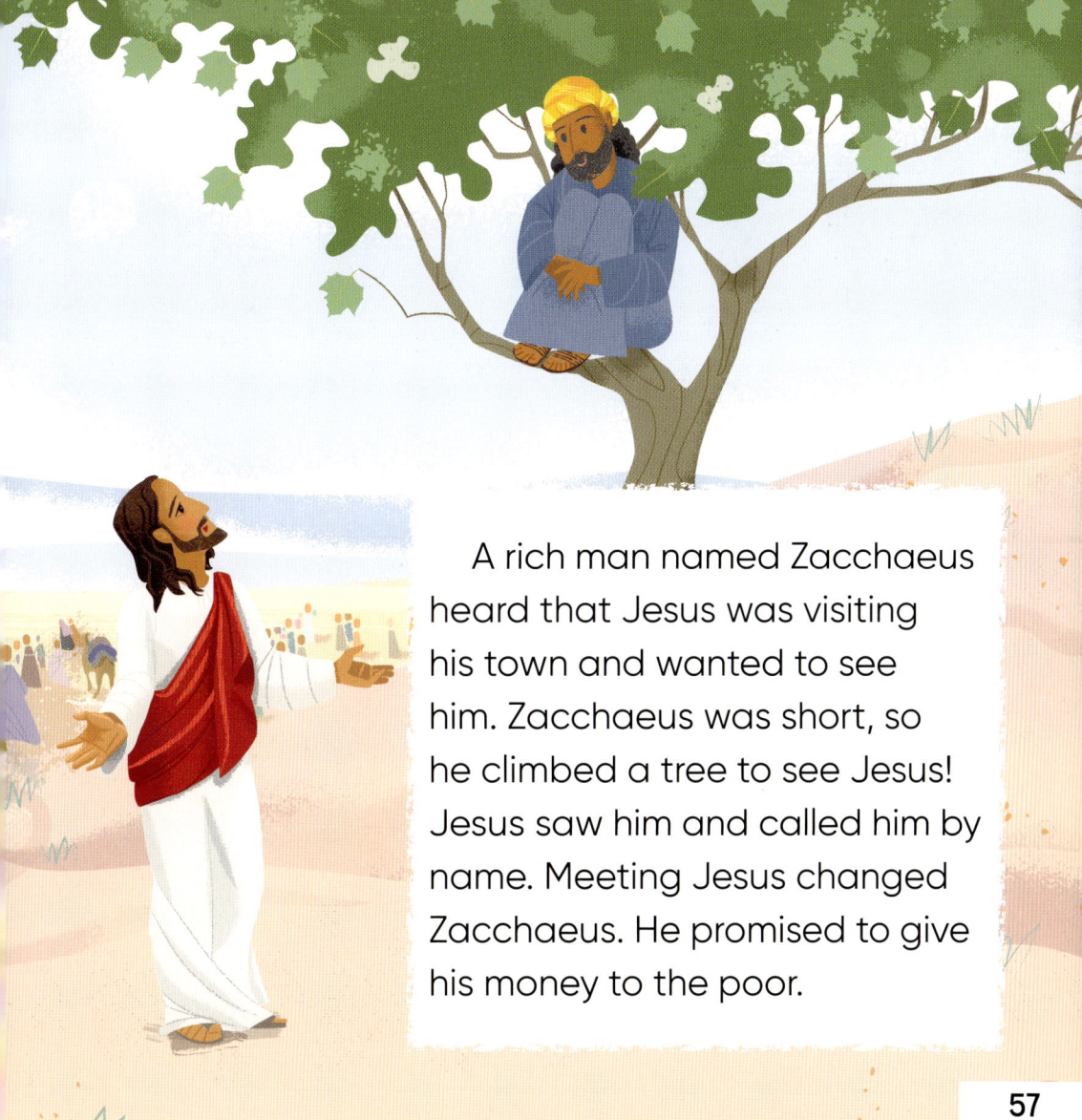

A rich man named Zacchaeus heard that Jesus was visiting his town and wanted to see him. Zacchaeus was short, so he climbed a tree to see Jesus! Jesus saw him and called him by name. Meeting Jesus changed Zacchaeus. He promised to give his money to the poor.

Nicodemus was a Pharisee, a Jewish leader. Jesus told Nicodemus that God loved the world so much that he sent his son to the world to save it.

Jesus visited a well in a city called Samaria. He talked with a woman he met at the well. He taught her about God. She ran back to her city and told them all about Jesus.

Children followed Jesus too! Some parents brought their children to Jesus for a blessing. The disciples said not to bother Jesus, but Jesus said he wanted to meet the children! He held them in his arms and blessed them.

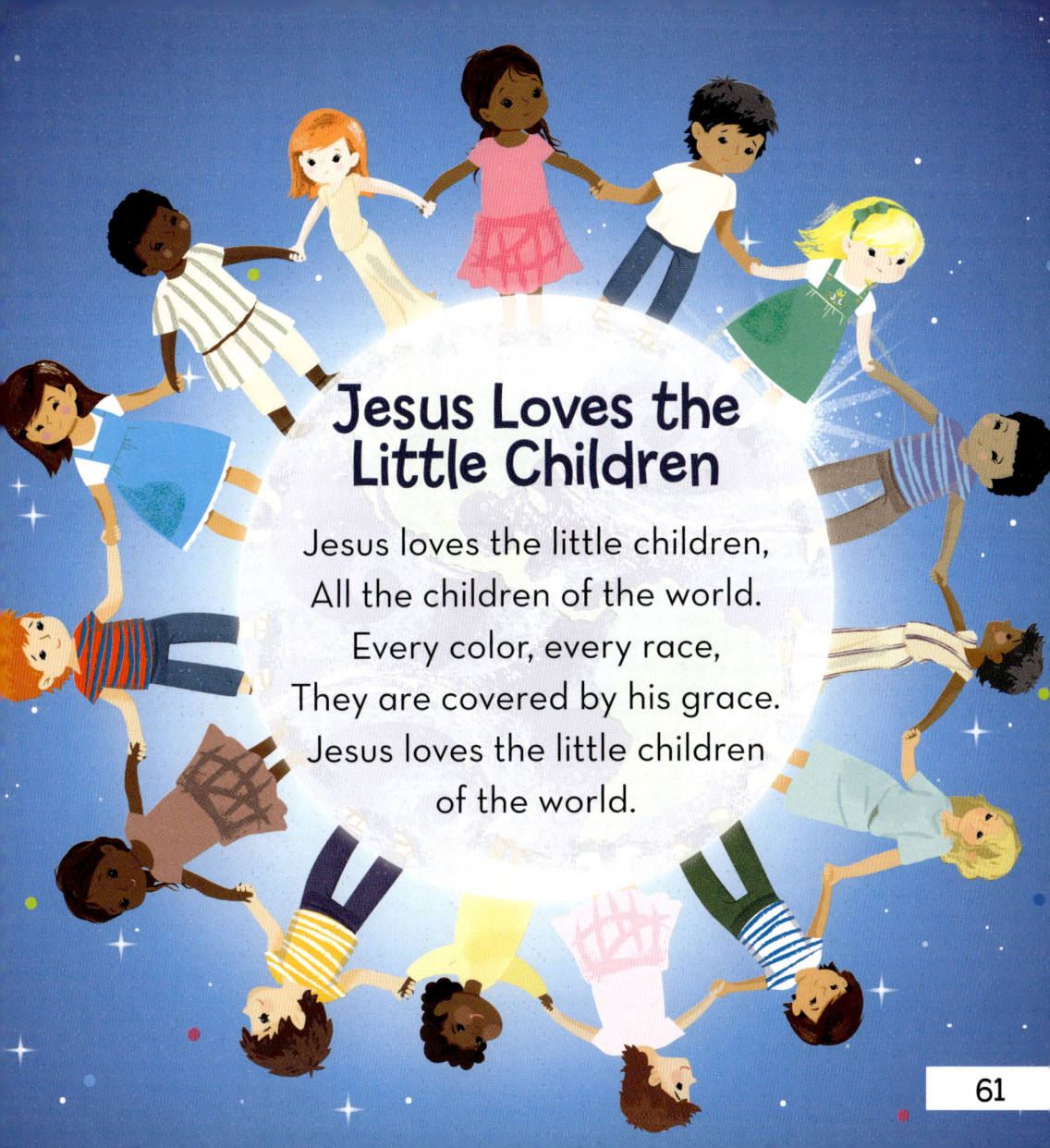

Jesus Loves Me

Jesus loves me, this I know,
For the Bible tells me so!
Little ones to him belong.
They are weak, but he is strong.

Yes, Jesus loves me!
Yes, Jesus loves me!
Yes, Jesus loves me!
The Bible tells me so.

O, the Deep, Deep Love of Jesus

O the deep, deep love of Jesus!
Vast, unmeasured, boundless, free,
Rolling as a mighty ocean
in its fullness over me.

Underneath me, all around me,
Is the current of thy love,
Leading onward, leading homeward,
To thy glorious rest above.

Since Jesus Came into My Heart

Since Jesus came into my heart,
Since Jesus came into my heart,
Floods of joy o'er my soul
like the sea billows roll,
Since Jesus came into my heart.

I Want Jesus to Walk with Me

I want Jesus to walk with me.
I want Jesus to walk with me.
All along my pilgrim journey,
Lord, I want Jesus to walk with me.

Jesus Teaches

One day Jesus went on a mountain and gave a sermon. He taught people how to live a good life.

"Blessed are the poor in spirit," Jesus said. "For theirs is the kingdom of heaven."

There were blessings for the meek, the merciful, the pure at heart, the peacemakers, and the persecuted.

Jesus called his followers the light of the world. "Let your light shine," Jesus said. "Let the world see your good works, which glorify God."

Jesus told them to treat other people like they would like to be treated. "Love your enemies," Jesus said.

Jesus told the people not to brag to other people about the good deeds they did or how much they prayed. Then he taught them a prayer. That prayer is called The Lord's Prayer, and we still pray it today!

The Lord's Prayer

Our Father which art in heaven,
Hallowed be thy name.
Thy kingdom come, thy will be done in earth,
As it is in heaven.
Give us this day our daily bread,
And forgive us our debts, as we forgive our debtors.
And lead us not into temptation, but deliver us from evil:
For thine is the kingdom,
And the power, and the glory, for ever.
Amen.

Every Time I Feel the Spirit

Every time I feel the Spirit
Moving in my heart, I will pray.
Yes, every time I feel the Spirit
Moving in my heart, I will pray.

Hear Us Pray

Grant us, Father, grace divine.

May thy smile upon us shine.

As we eat the broken bread,

Thine approval on us shed.

O How I Love Jesus

There is a name I love to hear,
I love to sing its worth.
It sounds like music in my ear,
The sweetest name on earth.

O how I love Jesus,
O how I love Jesus,
O how I love Jesus,
Because he first loved me!

What a Friend We Have in Jesus

What a friend we have in Jesus,

All our sins and griefs to bear!

What a privilege to carry

Everything to God in prayer!

O what peace we often forfeit,
O what needless pain we bear,
All because we do not carry
Everything to God in prayer!

The Parables

Jesus was a great storyteller. He used simple stories called parables to show people how to treat each other and to love God.

A shepherd had 100 sheep. One wandered away. He left his 99 sheep to look for his one lost sheep.

The shepherd was happier about finding one lost sheep than about the 99 who had not strayed. God is like the shepherd who cares for each member of his flock.

Jesus said that people who live by his teachings are like people who wisely build their homes on bedrock. A home built on solid rock can withstand even powerful storms.

But those who ignore his teachings are like foolish people who build their homes on sand. When a storm hits, a home built on sand will fall down with a mighty crash.

A Jewish man was traveling alone. Two thieves stole his money and beat him up. The man hoped someone would come along to help him.

A short time later, the man heard footsteps. It was a Jewish priest. Surely, he would help! But when he saw the injured man, the priest passed by without helping.

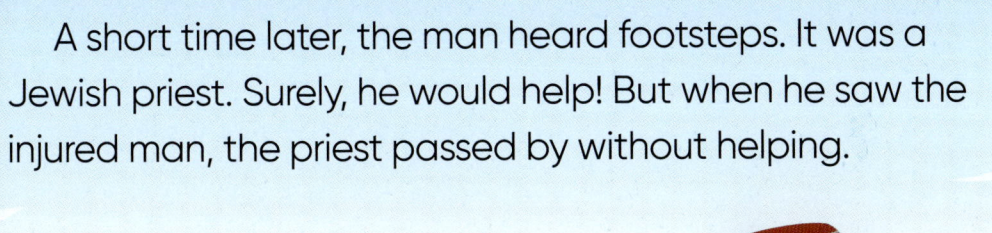

Later, the man heard footsteps again. It was a Levite, a Jewish temple assistant. When the Levite saw the injured man, he also passed by without helping.

Then the man saw a stranger from Samaria coming. Jewish people did not like Samaritans. Because the man was Jewish, he thought the Samaritan would pass by without helping.

The Samaritan stopped to help the injured man. He bandaged his wounds. The Samaritan took the man to an inn and cared for him all night.

Jesus explained that only the Samaritan followed God's command to love our neighbors. A neighbor can be anyone in need. We should follow the Samaritan's example and love others, even those we do not know or like.

A farmer scattered seeds in his field. Some of the seeds fell on the hard unplowed ground. Birds soon ate these exposed seeds.

Other seeds landed in the shallow, rocky soil and quickly sprouted. Because the plants did not have deep roots, the sun soon withered them.

Still other seeds fell among thorns and weeds. They choked the sun and water from the good seeds, so they died quickly.

The remaining seeds fell on good soil where they grew into a large crop. Jesus said the seeds are like God's message planted in our lives. Only those who truly accept it produce a great harvest.

A poor woman had only two coins. Instead of buying something for herself, she gave both coins to the church. She did this because she loved God.

Jesus said she gave more than the rich men who gave many coins. She gave all she had. But the rich men gave God only a small part of their money.

Jesus said that God's kingdom is like a tiny mustard seed that grows into a giant plant. Jesus was teaching how little things can become big things when God is behind them.

Jesus told a story about a prodigal son. There once was a man with two sons. They lived on a big farm.

The older son worked hard and always obeyed his father.

The younger son did not like to work. He wanted to travel and have fun.

One day the younger son said to his father, "Give me money so I can leave." His father agreed.

Shortly after that, the younger son packed his bags and left home. The older son stayed home to help with the farm.

The young man moved to a distant land, eager to spend his newfound wealth.

He wasted money on wild parties and sinful living. Soon all his money was gone. He had no money for food.

The only job he could find was feeding pigs. The young man was so hungry that even the pigs' food looked good to eat.

"Back home, even the servants have plenty of food," he thought. "Here I am starving!" Finally, the son came to understand his mistake.

"I will go home and ask Father for forgiveness," he thought. "I will ask him to hire me as a servant." The son left for home at once.

While he was still a long way off, the father saw his son approaching. He was filled with joy. The father ran to his son and hugged him.

"Forgive me, Father," the son said. "I have sinned against heaven and against you. I am no longer worthy of being called your son."

But the father welcomed his son home with open arms. "Bring my finest clothes and dress him," the father told his servants. "We will celebrate with a party!"

Meanwhile, the older son was working in the fields. When he returned home, he heard music and laughter. He asked a servant what was happening.

"Your father is throwing a party celebrating your brother's safe return," the servant said.

The older son was furious. The father came out and asked with him to join the party.

"I stayed here serving you all these years. Yet you never once threw me a party," the son said. "But when my brother comes home after wasting your money, you throw him a party!"

"You are always with me and everything I have is yours," the father said. "But your brother was lost and now he is found."

Just like the father in the story, God always welcomes us home again.

The King of Love My Shepherd Is

The King of love my shepherd is,
Whose goodness fail me never.
I nothing lack if I am his,
And he is mine forever.

My Shepherd Will Supply My Need

My Shepherd, you supply my need,
Most holy is your name.
In pastures fresh you make me feed,
Beside the living stream.

Blessed Assurance, Jesus Is Mine

This is my story, this is my song,

Praising my Savior all the day long.

This is my story, this is my song,

Praising my Savior all the day long.

Jesus Is the Sweetest Name I Know

Jesus is the sweetest name I know,

And he's just the same as his lovely name,

And that's the reason why I love him so.

Oh, Jesus is the sweetest name I know.

Praise God from Whom All Blessings Flow

Praise God, from whom all blessings flow.
Praise him, all creatures here below.
Praise him above, ye heavenly host.
Praise Father, Son, and Holy Ghost.

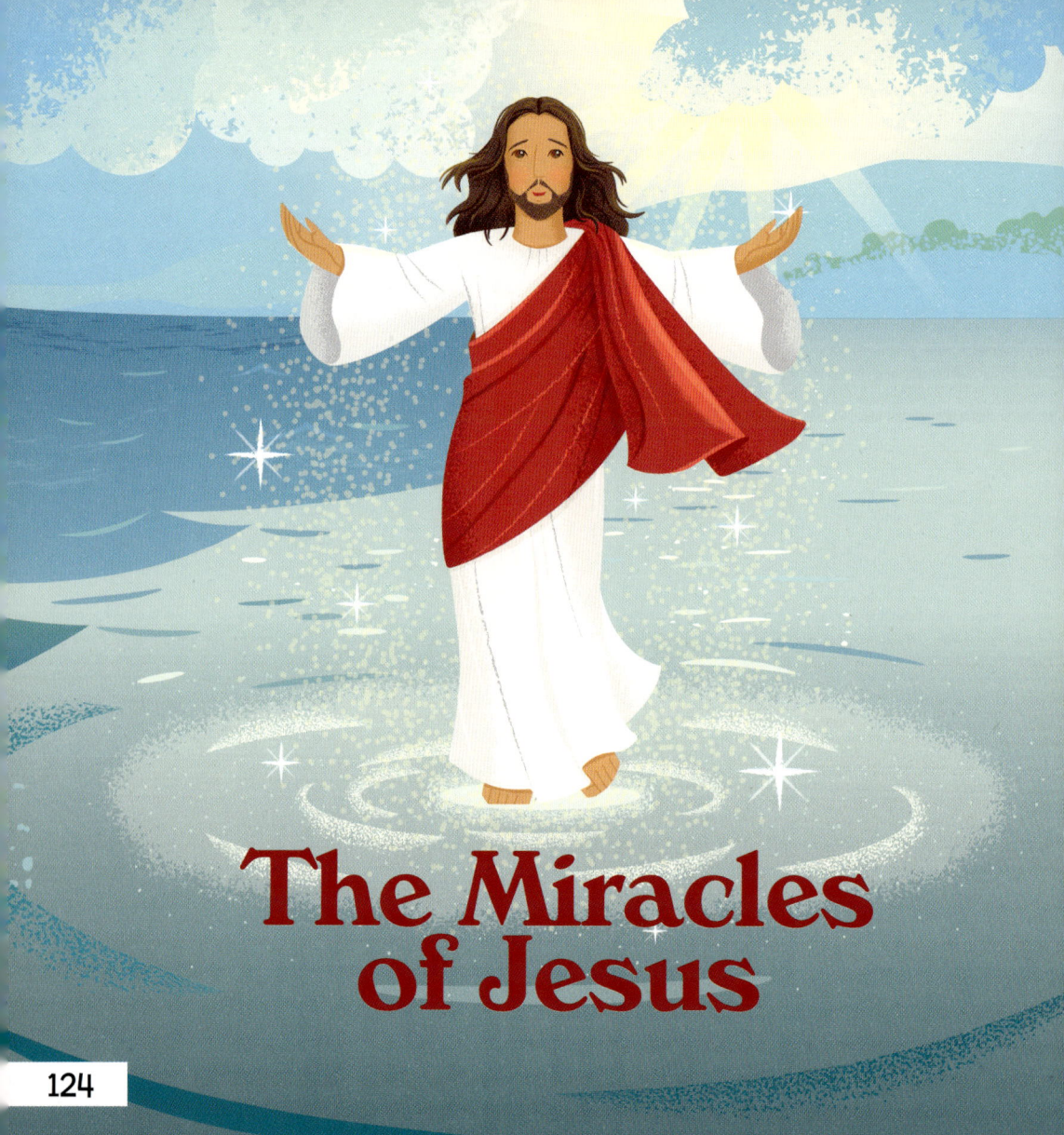

Jesus performed many miracles. He turned water into wine, controlled nature, healed the sick, and even raised people from the dead. These miracles showed that Jesus was God's son.

Jesus performed his first miracle at a wedding in Cana. Jesus's mother, Mary, was one of the guests. Mary told Jesus that the hosts had run out of wine.

Jesus had a plan. There were six empty jugs sitting nearby.

"Fill these with water," Jesus told the servants.

The servants filled the jugs with water.

"Now take a cup to the host and ask him to taste it," Jesus told one of the servants.

The servant did as she was told. The host was amazed. "This is the best wine I have ever tasted," he said.

On a boat trip across a lake with his disciples, Jesus fell fast asleep. Suddenly a great storm arose. The disciples were afraid the boat would sink. They woke Jesus.

"Help us!" they cried.

Jesus said to the storm, "Peace, be still." And it was. "Who is this?" the disciples asked. "Even the winds and the waves obey him."

One day some men carried their friend who could not walk to a house where Jesus was teaching. They could not find a way in because of the crowd.

They climbed up on the roof and lowered their friend down in front of Jesus. When Jesus saw their faith, he said to the paralyzed man, "Friend, your sins are forgiven."

This made the priests and elders upset.

"Only God can forgive sins!" one said.

Jesus responded, "I will prove I have the power on Earth to forgive sins."

Then Jesus said to the paralyzed man, "Stand up, take your mat, and walk. You are healed."
The man immediately stood up and walked.

Jesus traveled to many places teaching about God. One day, a giant crowd gathered to listen to him. The crowd was hungry, but there was not enough food to feed everyone.

A boy gave five loaves of bread and two fish to Jesus. Then Jesus changed the bread and fish into enough food to feed everyone.

The disciples were out at sea when a storm began battering their boat. From a hilltop, Jesus could see that his disciples were in danger.

Jesus walked on the water toward the boat. The disciples were frightened.

"Do not be afraid," Jesus said.

"You really are the Son of God!" they exclaimed.

Jesus's friends Mary and Martha had a brother, Lazarus. Lazarus got sick and died. A few days after his death, Jesus came to see the sisters. The sisters took Jesus to their brother's tomb.

"Roll the stone away," Jesus told them.

At first, they did not want to. Lazarus had been dead for four days. But Jesus insisted. So they rolled the stone away.

"Lazarus, come out," Jesus said.
Then Lazarus came out of the tomb alive again!

Now Thank We All Our God

Now thank we all our God
With heart and hands and voices,
Who wondrous things has done,
In whom his world rejoices,
Who from our mothers' arms
Has blessed us on our way
With countless gifts of love,
And still is ours today.

Jesus Is a Rock in a Weary Land

Jesus is a rock in a weary land,

A weary land, a weary land.

My Jesus is a rock in a weary land,

A shelter in the time of storm.

Turn Your Eyes Upon Jesus

Turn your eyes upon Jesus,
Look full in his wonderful face,
And the things of earth will grow strangely dim,
In the light of his glory and grace.

Jesus Saves

We have heard the joyful sound.
Jesus saves! Jesus saves!
Spread the tidings all around.
Jesus saves! Jesus saves!

Bear the news to every land,
Climb the steeps and cross the waves,
Onward! 'Tis our Lord's command.
Jesus saves! Jesus saves!

Jesus Saves Us

Jesus and his disciples went to Jerusalem for the feast of Passover.
Some people were very happy to see Jesus.
They praised Jesus, waving palm branches and crying, "Hosanna! Blessed is the King!" Other people were not very happy that Jesus was being called a king. They decided to get rid of Jesus.

When Jesus knew that he would die, he gathered all his disciples for one last meal that was very special. He told them to remember him.

Jesus was put to death on the cross and buried in a tomb. When Mary Magdalene, Jesus's mother Mary, and another woman went to visit the tomb, they found it empty! Jesus had risen from the dead!

Jesus's followers told everyone that Jesus was the Son of God! A man named Saul did not believe this. He hated Jesus's followers. One day while he was on the road, he saw a bright light and fell to the ground!

He heard the voice of Jesus. After that day, Saul was called Paul and spread the word of God everywhere!

When I Survey the Wondrous Cross

When I survey the wondrous cross

On which the Prince of glory died,

My richest gain I count but loss,

And pour contempt on all my pride.

Jesus Paid It All

Jesus paid it all,
All to him I owe.
Sin had left a crimson stain,
He washed it white as snow.

In the Garden

I come to the garden alone,
While the dew is still on the roses.
And the voice I hear, falling on my ear,
The Son of God discloses.

And he walks with me, and he talks with me,
And he tells me I am his own,
And the joy we share as we tarry there,
None other has ever known.

Jesus Christ Is Risen Today

Jesus Christ is risen today, Alleluia!
Our triumphant holy day, Alleluia!
Who did once upon the cross, Alleluia!
Suffer to redeem our loss. Alleluia!

Hymns of praise then let us sing, Alleluia!
Unto Christ, our heavenly King, Alleluia!
Who endured the cross and grave, Alleluia!
Sinners to redeem and save. Alleluia!

I Love to Tell the Story

I love to tell the story,

Of unseen things above,

Of Jesus and his glory,

Of Jesus and his love.